THIS WALKER BOOK BELONGS TO:

_____

_____

_____

_____

For John Mitchell
and Floss

First published 1992 by Walker Books Ltd
87 Vauxhall Walk, London SE11 5HJ

This edition published 1993

12 14 15 13 11

© 1992 Kim Lewis

This book has been typeset in Sabon.

Printed in Hong Kong/China

British Library Cataloguing in Publication Data
A catalogue record for this book is
available from the British Library.

ISBN 0-7445-2071-1

Floss

Kim Lewis

WALKER BOOKS

AND SUBSIDIARIES

LONDON • BOSTON • SYDNEY

Floss was a young Border collie, who belonged to an old man in a town. She walked with the old man in the streets, and loved playing ball with children in the park.

"My son is a farmer,"
  the old man told Floss.
"He has a sheepdog
  who is too old to work.
  He needs a young dog
  to herd sheep on his farm.
  He could train a
  Border collie like you."

So Floss and the old man
travelled, away from
the town with
its streets and houses
and children playing ball
in the park.
They came to the
heather-covered hills
of a valley, where nothing
much grew except sheep.

Somewhere in her
memory, Floss knew
about sheep.
Old Nell soon showed
her how to round them up.
The farmer trained her
to run wide and lie down,
to walk on behind,
to shed, and to pen.
She worked very hard
to become a good sheepdog.

But sometimes Floss
woke up at night,
while Nell lay sound asleep.
She remembered
about playing with
children and rounding up
balls in the park.

The farmer took Floss
on the hill one day,
to see if she could gather
the sheep on her own.
She was rounding them
up when she heard a sound.
At the edge of the field
the farmer's children were
playing, with a brand new
black and white ball.

Floss remembered
all about children.
She ran to play with
their ball. She showed
off her best nose kicks,
her best passes. She
did her best springs
in the air.
"Hey, Dad, look at this!"
yelled the children.
"Look at Floss!"
The sheep started
drifting away.

The sheep escaped
through the gate and
into the yard. There
were sheep in the garden
and sheep on the road.
"FLOSS! LIE DOWN!"
The farmer's voice
was like thunder.
"You are meant for
work on this farm,
not play!"
He took Floss back to
the dog house.

Floss lay and worried
about balls and sheep.
She dreamt about
the streets of a town,
the hills of a valley,
children and farmers,
all mixed together,
while Nell had to round
up the straying sheep.

But Nell was too old
to work every day,
and Floss had to learn to
take her place.
She worked so hard
to gather sheep well,
she was much too tired
to dream any more.
The farmer was
pleased and ran Floss
in the dog trials.
"She's a good worker now,"
the old man said.

The children still wanted
to play with their ball.
"Hey, Dad," they asked,
"can Old Nell play now?"
But Nell didn't know
about children and play.
"No one can play ball
like Floss," they said.
"Go on, then," whispered
the farmer to Floss.
The children kicked the
ball high in the air.

Floss remembered
all about children.
She ran to play with
their ball.
She showed off her
best nose kicks,
her best passes.
She did her best
springs in the air.

MORE WALKER PAPERBACKS
For You to Enjoy
Also by Kim Lewis

THE SHEPHERD BOY

Shortlisted for the 1991 Kate Greenaway Medal

Through the changing seasons, James watches his farmer father
at work and cannot wait for the day when he can be a farmer too.

"Illustrations that make you want to stroke the page, and a story of such family
warmth and country charm you're left with a warm glow." *Books for Keeps*

0-7445-1762-1   £4.99

EMMA'S LAMB

When Emma's dad brings a small lamb into the house at lambing time, Emma tries to look after it.

"Unsentimental and with wonderfully detailed pictures … special." *Valerie Bierman, The Scotsman*

0-7445-2031-2   £4.99

FIRST SNOW

Sara goes with Mummy, teddy and the dogs to feed the sheep one
winter's morning and to her delight, it starts to snow.

"A delightful book for parents and younger children to share and for older
children to linger over." *Children's Books of the Year*

ISBN 0-7445-4325-8   £4.99

Walker Paperbacks are available from most booksellers, or by post from B.B.C.S., P.O. Box 941, Hull, North Humberside HU1 3YQ

24 hour telephone credit card line 01482 224626

To order, send: Title, author, ISBN number and price for each book ordered, your full name and address,
cheque or postal order payable to BBCS for the total amount and allow the following for postage and packing:
UK and BFPO: £1.00 for the first book, and 50p for each additional book to a maximum of £3.50.
Overseas and Eire: £2.00 for the first book, £1.00 for the second and 50p for each additional book.

Prices and availability are subject to change without notice.